Hey Little Baby!

Heather Leigh • Illustrated by Geneviève Côté

Palatine Public Library District
700 N. North Court
Palatine, IL 60067-8159

PALATINE PUBLIC LIBRARY

P9-DHI-774

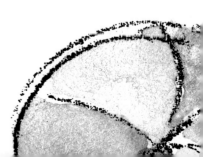

For my son Azier
—H. L.

For Adrien and Henri, cousins and princes
—G. C.

BEACH LANE BOOKS • An imprint of Simon & Schuster Children's Publishing Division • 1230 Avenue of the Americas, New York, New York 10020 • Text copyright © 2012 by Heather Leigh • Illustrations copyright © 2012 by Geneviève Côté • All rights reserved, including the right of reproduction in whole or in part in any form. • BEACH LANE BOOKS is a trademark of Simon & Schuster, Inc. • For information about special discounts for bulk purchases, please contact Simon & Schuster Special Sales at 1-866-506-1949 or business@simonandschuster.com. • The Simon & Schuster Speakers Bureau can bring authors to your live event. For more information or to book an event, contact the Simon & Schuster Speakers Bureau at 1-866-248-3049 or visit our website at www.simonspeakers.com. • Book design by Lauren Rille • The text for this book is set in Museo. • The illustrations for this book are rendered in mixed media. • Manufactured in China • 0112 SCP • First Edition • 1 2 3 4 5 6 7 8 9 10 • Library of Congress Cataloging-in-Publication Data • Leigh, Heather, 1968– • Hey little baby! / by Heather Leigh ; illustrated by Geneviève Côté.—1st ed. • p. cm. • Summary: Welcomes a new baby into the world with thoughts of what it might accomplish in life. • ISBN 978-1-4169-8979-0 (hardcover) • [1. Babies—Fiction.] I. Côté, Geneviève, ill. II. Title. • PZ7.L53323He 2012 [E]—dc22 • 2010001311

Hey little baby,
you've arrived in our world.

What will you find in this world?

What will you find in this marvelous world?

Hey little baby,
you've found your hands.

What will you make
with those hands?

What will you make with those beautiful hands?

Hey little baby,
you've found your feet.

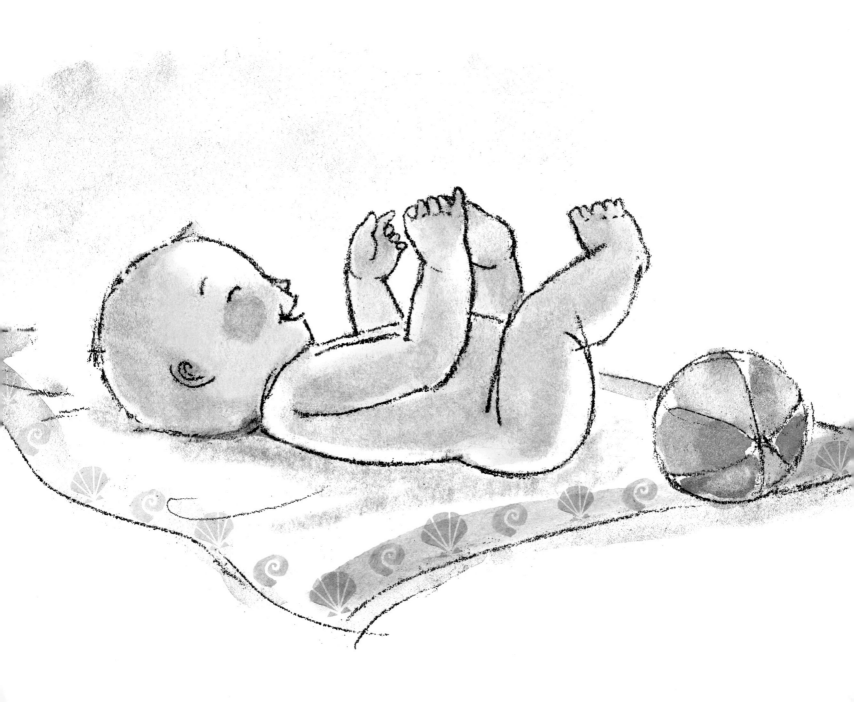

Where will you go with those feet?

Where will you go with those adorable feet?

Hey little baby,
you've found your nose.

What will you smell with that nose?

What will you smell with that darling nose?

Hey little baby,
you've found your mouth.

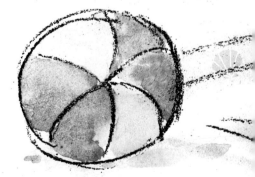

What will you taste
with that mouth?

What will you taste with
that delightful mouth?

Hey little baby,
you've found your voice.

How will you use that voice?

How will you use that lovely voice?

Hey little baby,
you've arrived in our world.

Who will you be in this world?

Who will you be in this marvelous world?

We can't wait to find out!